JAMES BEAR'S PIE

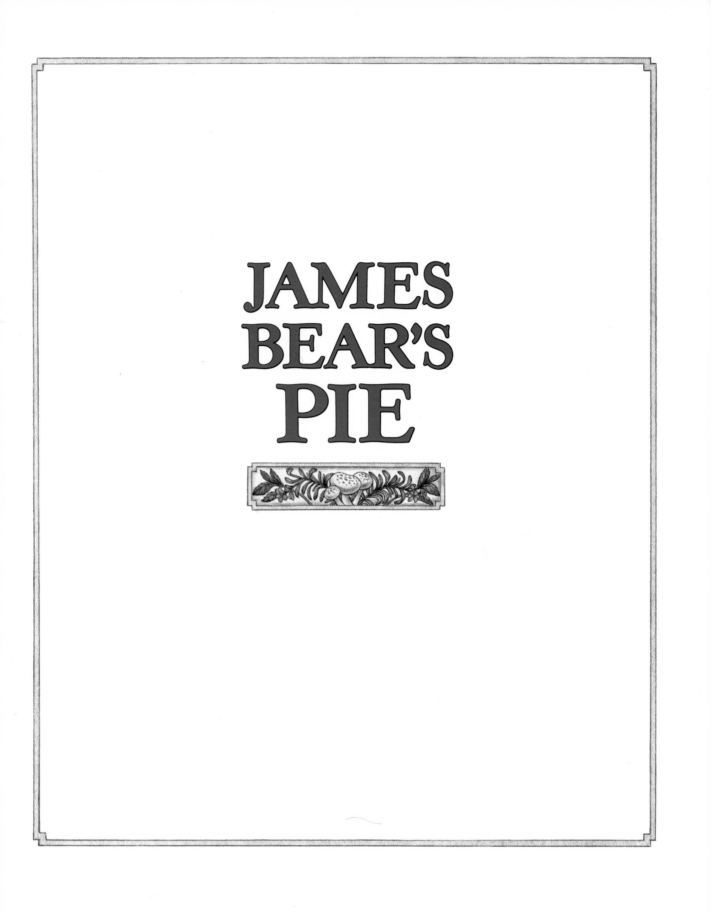

For Ruth Virginia
and Dorothy Alice
—J.L.

For my parents, Rose and Nick Franco
—B.F-F.

Charles Scribner's Sons Books for Young Readers
Macmillan Publishing Company • 866 Third Avenue, New York, NY 10022
Maxwell Macmillan Canada, Inc.
1200 Eglinton Avenue East, Suite 200, Don Mills, Ontario M3C 3N1

Macmillan Publishing Company is part of the
Maxwell Communication Group of Companies.

First edition   Printed in Hong Kong   10 9 8 7 6 5 4 3 2 1

Library of Congress Cataloging-in-Publication Data
Latimer, Jim, 1943–
James Bear's pie / Jim Latimer.—1st ed.   p.   cm.
Summary: Bear's animal friends try to rescue him
when he becomes trapped in his giant, freshly baked pie.
[1. Cookery—Fiction.   2. Bears—Fiction.   3. Animals—Fiction.]
I. Title.   ISBN 0-684-19226-8
PZ7.L369617 Jam   1992   [E]—dc20   90–36193   CIP   AC

JAMES BEAR'S PIE

JIM LATIMER

Pictures by
Betsy Franco-Feeney

CHARLES SCRIBNER'S SONS • NEW YORK

Maxwell Macmillan Canada • Toronto
Maxwell Macmillan International
New York • Oxford • Singapore • Sydney

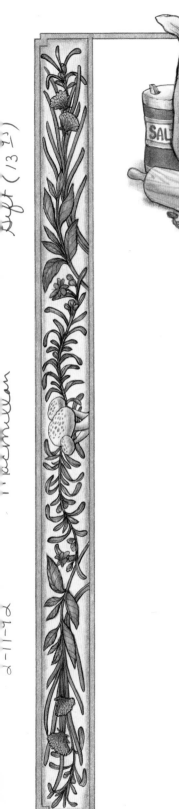

James Bear was a solitary, cider-colored, heavy-pawed animal who wandered the hills and prairies, foraging for herbs and flowers. He rarely entered the deep woods and seldom met other animals, apart from the ragged geese and short-tempered crickets who were his neighbors. But Bear's favorite animal when he met her—his best friend —was Skunk. Technically Jasmine Iris Laurel Chrysanthemum, Bear's friend was mostly known as Skunk.

Skunk lived in a forest of maple trees, and she was a collector. She collected parts of clocks and broken bells, also picture frames and parachutes and pencil leads—found objects, she called them; and when Bear came upon a found object or when he stumbled over one, he usually brought it to his friend. And Skunk often came out to the hills or prairies to look for Bear—usually to recite to him, for she was a collector *and* a memorizer. Skunk memorized poems and verses, specializing in parts of popular songs—songs she remembered from her found radio.

Once, Skunk came to look for Bear to recite a verse about a bicycle. Bear was wading through a sea of blue stems when Skunk found him. She watched from a distance, from the brow of a low hill, as Bear trampled the tall grass around him. He seemed to be trampling *figures* in the grass. Circles. And spirals. And—Skunk couldn't quite see—shamrocks, maybe. She shook her head. What was he up to, she wondered. Then, realizing she had forgotten her song (it had taken that long to find the wandering bear), she made her way down to the tall grass.

"Bear," she shouted.

Bear stopped trampling. He turned and stared. When he saw Skunk peering at him from the bunched blue grass, his eyes brightened.

"I had a song for you," she told him. "A good one," she said. "But I forgot it while I was looking for you."

Bear was crestfallen. "Well, never mind," he said. "It will come back to you. Besides," he added, "I was just coming to look for *you*."

"Have you found anything?" Skunk asked him, thinking of her collection.

Bear sighed. "No," he told her. "I am just tired of this fibery grass, this—*alfalfa*." Bear dismissed the tall, blue grass with a sweep of his paw. "I have decided to try something else—decided to *make* something else. Something with more protein and more calories than grass. Something with more *taste*. What do you think?"

Skunk thought about it. "You could make a pie," she ventured. Skunk

considered a moment. "I don't have an oven," she told Bear, "but Crow has one."

Crow (technically, Aloysius Crow) lived atop an oven in the old bakery at the edge of the forest. Crow was also a collector, a collector and a scientist, and Skunk was pretty sure he had a cookbook. That settled the question for Bear. Skunk decided that a soybean pie, raisin flavored, would be good and would have protein, and Bear agreed. They turned away from the tall grass and set out together in search of Crow.

They found him perched atop his oven, poring over a textbook about astronomy.

"You see," Crow began when he saw them, "collapsed stars, sometimes called *white dwarfs*—" But Skunk interrupted him. Crow loved science and he loved to talk. He was *didactic,* which means that he was always trying to teach somebody something, and when he got started, it was almost impossible to stop him talking.

"Can Bear use your oven?" Skunk asked him. "He's going to bake a pie."

Crow tilted his head toward Skunk. "Bear is going to bake a pie?" he asked, astonished. As far as Crow could remember, no one had used his oven for many years. "I thought Bear ate grass," he said.

"I'm tired of it," Bear answered.

Crow seemed to ponder this, inclining his head toward Bear and bristling the feathers above his brow. "You're tired," he said. Bear nodded.

"He needs something with protein," Skunk explained. "Something with *more* protein," she said.

"Something with more protein." Crow cleared his throat, apparently appreciating Bear's dilemma. "Certainly," he said. "Certainly Bear may use my oven." Crow blinked and paused. "Let me see," he said. "I think I have a cookbook. *And* flour. And—what else do you put in a pie? Yeast. I have a lot of yeast. You may use it all."

"Do you have any raisins?" Skunk asked him.

Crow did not have raisins. Or soybeans. But he had a rolling pin and a mixing bowl and a baking pan, a round baking pan almost fifty inches across and only a little dented. Skunk went to look for soybeans and raisins while Crow assembled all of these things.

"What do you think?" he asked Bear proudly when he had gathered his collection about him.

Bear took a close look at Crow's cookbook. It said

BREAD,
Whole Grain

Inside there were recipes for seven-grain bread. For nine- and eleven-grain. Bear looked at a chapter called "Flour," looked at lists of wheat flours and ryes, oatmeal flours and barleys. There were breads baked with basil, Bear saw, and fennel-flavored bread and—he shuddered. There was a bread made from *alfalfa*.

"Do you have any pie cookbooks?" Bear asked Crow.

Crow's expression was blank. He did not have a pie cookbook. He had no other cookbooks. For a moment, Crow was confounded—but only for a moment.

Crow flapped down from his oven, landing deftly between Bear's ears. He squinted at the bread cookbook. "You could make a bread-crust pie." Crow inclined his head, pointing with a primary feather. "A bread piecrust," he said.

Bear stared up at him.

"For example," Crow said, "pizza is pie—*and* bread."

Bear had never heard of pizza.

"Stuffed pizza," Crow told him. "Let's say raisin-and-soybean-stuffed, bread-crust pizza."

Bear was impressed with the sound of this.

"Now," Crow concluded, consulting his watch, "go right ahead." Crow had an afternoon appointment, but he invited Bear to feel free to bake his pie.

"You have everything you need." Crow glanced about, making sure. "And we'll set the oven for four hundred degrees." Crow set the oven. "I will come back to see how you get on, and I trust Skunk will be back soon."

Bear found a recipe he liked. Plain white flour (it said), warm water, salt, molasses, oil, and yeast—two fresh cakes.

Bear followed the directions, tripling the recipe and reading aloud.

"First sift together the salt and the flour," he read, and he did this. "Now crush two cakes of new, fresh yeast in warm water." Bear squinted at the book. He looked at Crow's yeast. Thirty-six cakes—one case. The words STONE "YEAST" were printed on the box in large letters, "YEAST" in quotation marks. Below, in smaller letters, Bear read, "Strong mineral leavening, made from sulphates and phosphates of certain minerals, and from plenty of plain baking powder." James Bear stared at the box. He did not know what sulphates or phosphates were. He did not know why the word "YEAST" was printed with quotation marks. The box said this "strong yeast" had been "compounded by Crow." It said, "For best results, use before July." Bear blinked. *This* was July, he was pretty sure. July or later. Possibly it was August or September.

One case of Stone yeast, crushed, and a little baking soda and baking powder left room in Crow's bowl for oil, molasses, water, and a little flour and salt. These things mixed to a damp glue. Disappointment crept into Bear's eyes as he stirred, but gradually the glue turned to dough, and it was at this moment that Skunk returned with her beans and raisins.

She had remembered her bicycle song, but Bear's dough was so striking that the song went out of her head again.

"Bear," she said, "it looks good."

Bear divided the dough with his friend.

Each kneaded half, traded, and kneaded half again. When it was smooth, Bear rolled his half of the dough on a board and lined Crow's pan with it. Skunk and Bear then filled the pie with raisins, beans, and a little parsley, and covered it with Skunk's half of the dough.

"Perfect." Bear beamed at his friend and thought a moment. He decided the geese and the crickets, his neighbors, would want to see the pie. "The geese will want to see it," he said. "And the crickets."

"I will go and get them," Skunk told him. "Just wait." But then Skunk thought better of this. "No, don't wait," she said. "You should try the pie when it's ready." Bear blinked at her. "It's for you," she told him.

When Skunk had gone, Bear lifted the pie into Crow's oven and settled himself to wait, but it did not take long. As the oven timer ticked toward zero, a raisiny, bakery smell billowed through Crow's corner of the forest. The smell was pungent. Powerful. Compared to tall grass, it was wonderfully savory.

And then the timer dinged. Bear rose to his feet, opened the oven door, peered in, and stood back. He staggered. Bear *was* staggered, for the sight that greeted him was staggering.

The pie had grown, had risen to almost twice its original size, and yet as Bear lifted it from the oven, it seemed strangely light. In fact, a beautiful, honey-colored crust had risen and was still rising—gradually but very steadily. Now that it was in the open, it seemed massive, and its smell, rich and warm and raisiny, was almost overwhelming. Bear lifted his nose skyward, closed his eyes, and for a long moment, he sniffed in silence. And as he sniffed, the pie grew. It grew larger and still larger. It did not stop growing.

When Bear opened his eyes at last, the pie had grown to almost his own size, and it seemed to beckon to him to take a bite.

Rising to his full height, James Bear began to circle the pie, searching for a likely place. He circled to the left, then back to the right, and then planting his feet firmly and reaching in, he got hold of the honey-colored crust.

The crust crackled. It steamed. Bear tasted—raisins. Soybeans and molasses. Baking powder and a little parsley. "Perfect," he said. Could there be anything as perfect as raisin pie? His eyes said plainly, "No."

Bear tried a second piece of the pie, and this time the effect was most evident in his ears. They flickered with pleasure. By his fifth piece, the cider-colored bear had assumed a dreamy expression, and yet, had he been more alert, had he been only a little more attentive, Bear might have seen that the more he ate of the pie, the more pie there was to eat. By his seventh piece, it had grown larger than himself. By his eleventh piece, the pie seemed almost to surround him.

Skunk, meanwhile, had found Bear's geese and his crickets. The geese were following her now toward Crow's corner. (The crickets had proven so unruly, they could not be persuaded to come.) As the geese hustled and flapped beside her, Skunk was giving them a lively account of the making of the pie, exaggerating a little to prompt their curiosity.

Skunk recited the recipe from memory, listing ingredients and directions, until she came to the part about yeast. Two cakes of fresh yeast in warm water. Skunk said this aloud and was suddenly stricken. *Two* cakes. Bear had used thirty-six cakes of "strong Stone 'yeast'"—*eighteen times too many.*

Skunk's eyes were filled with fright. "We must hurry," she whispered to the geese. "Bear is in danger."

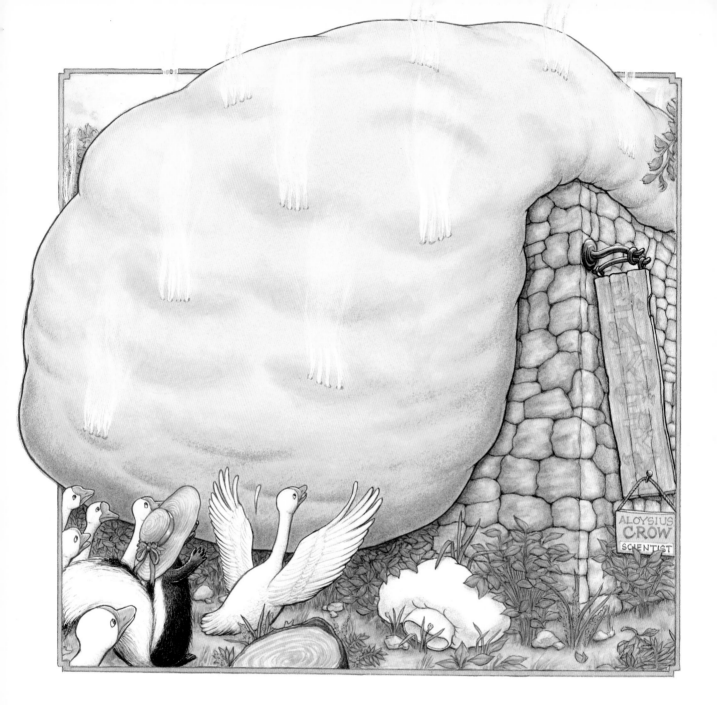

Bear was. The pie had engulfed him. It had grown, gradually but steadily, and now completely surrounded him. Bear was folded *inside* the pie. When Skunk and the geese reached Crow's corner, they were greeted by a hill of pastry, a crust out of control. And Bear was nowhere to be seen.

"Geese," Skunk shouted, "Bear is *in* the pie. You must help. We must get him out."

Skunk saw immediately what had to be done. Like a striped field marshal, she mustered the geese into ranks, aimed their bills at the pie, and signaled "Charge."

Together the geese (twenty-three of them) flew toward the pie, bills leveled, eyes blazing, and together they struck the pie's shell.

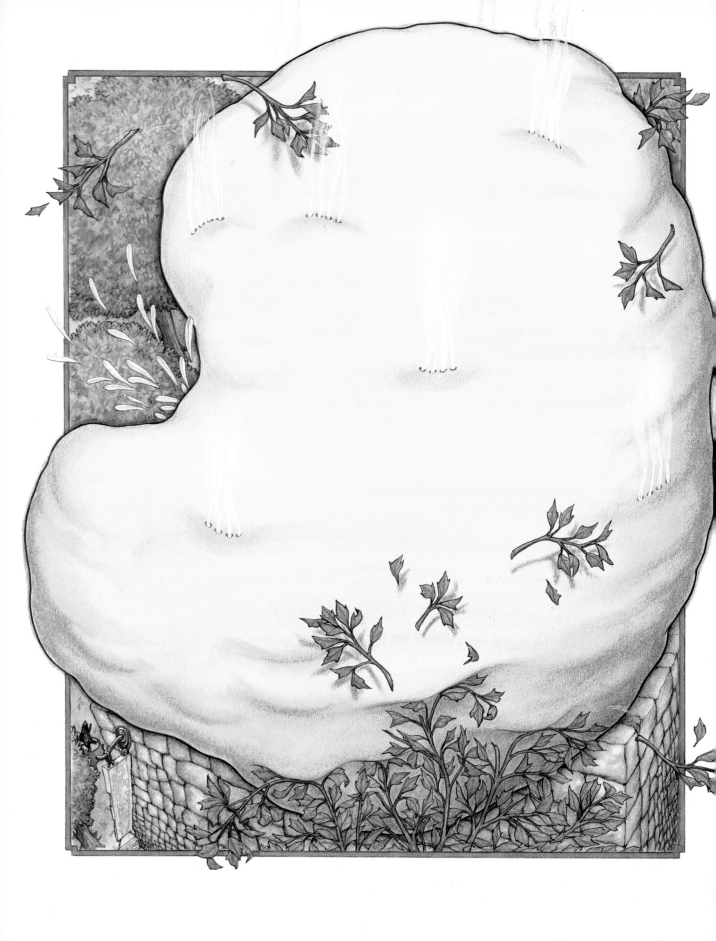

The impact was terrible. Crow's corner rang with a sound like the battering of drums. The pie bulged, it ballooned, but it did not break. The geese's bills were too blunt. The pie's shell was too tough. Bear was still locked inside.

Then Crow came home.

"Crow," Skunk shouted, "Bear's pie will not stop rising. He used a *whole case* of yeast."

"But," Crow stammered, staring at the pie, "but baking stops yeast from working." Crow was almost speechless with astonishment. "Baking *kills* yeast," he said.

"Not *Stone* yeast," Skunk told him. "Not your *mineral* yeast. Not *thirty-six cakes*. Crow, Bear is *in* the pie. We cannot get him out."

Crow tilted his head at the pie, which had grown so large, it was breaking the branches of trees.

Crow's eyebrows frilled. The feathers around his neck bristled. His bill was *not* blunt. He brandished it now, opened his great black wings, and lifted himself up over the heads of the geese and Skunk. Crow's wings beat the air like propeller blades. He rose to a great height above the pie, then collapsed his wings and stooped down. Crow hurtled toward the pie, shearing the air like a missile.

"Be careful," Skunk whispered, her eyes wide with anxiety, but she needn't have worried. Crow placed his point perfectly. His bill breached the pie and pierced it through—well to one side of Bear—and the report of its impact was like a pistol shot. The golden crust collapsed, releasing a cloud of mineral yeast gas, and there, amid a wreckage of raisins, was Bear, with eyes closed, nose skyward.

"Wonderful," he said. Bear looked hugely satisfied. Crow and Skunk and the geese bit their tongues to keep from laughing. "Perfect," said the pale, cider-colored bear, and added, "I will never go back to alfalfa."